# Snoopy's Land of Make Believe

Snoopy's Imagination Carries Him Away

Based on the comic strip "Peanuts"
Created and Written by:
Charles M. Schulz

Produced and Directed by:
Lee Mendelson
Desirée Goyette

Original Music and Lyrics by:
Desirée Goyette

Music Arranged and Conducted by:
Ed Bogas

Art Director:
Frank Hill

## "Land of Make-Believe"

Where do rainbows glow?
Where do fairy tales grow?
In the land of make-believe!
Where are nursery rhymes?
Where is "once upon a time"?
In the land of make-believe!!

When you make believe, you can weave
A story all your own
You're a bird in flight or a shining knight
Who pulls a sword from out of a stone

Where does magic dwell?
Where do witches find a spell?
In the land of make-believe
Where can princes glide?
In the land of make-believe

Oh yes you can be
Anything, you see
When you make believe
In the land of make-believe

You can find a daydream
Make a fantasy come true
If you just make believe
It soon becomes a part of you

Oh yes you can be
Anything, you see
When you make believe
In the land of make-believe

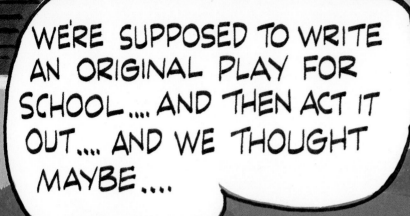

"I'm Gonna Be A Star"

I'm gonna be a star, I'll be the best by far
And everyone in town will know my name
And all the kids in class will want my autograph
I'll live a life that's full of glamour and fame

Like Rin-Tin-Tin or Lassie
That's what I'd like to be
I'll be the biggest beagle-star
In all of his-tor-y!!

A beautiful girl with golden hair
And satin gowns with lace
I'll be so very lovely that
You'll never forget my face!!

The handsome hero, bold and brave
That's the role I'd choose
I'd stand and fight for victory
And never—ever—lose!!!!!

I'm gonna have my name in the paper at school
A princess...A knight...
Joe Cool!
That's what I'll be...
When...When...When...
Anybody passes me on the street they'll whisper
    "Is that who I think it is?" and I'll say
    "Yes, it's me"

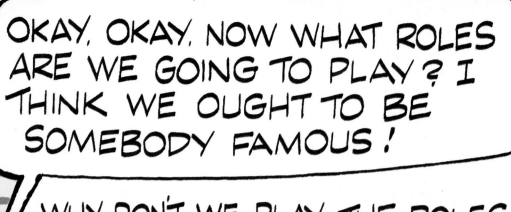

## "I'm Just A Simple Dog"

I'm just a simple dog
Who likes a pat on the head
I'm just a simple dog
Who hates to get out of bed
Give me some toast and tea...and a little T.V.
A simple dog...that's me!

I'm just a simple dog
Why should I go and fetch?
I'd rather lie on my house
And yawn and stretch
Give me some toast and tea...and a little T.V.
A simple dog...that's me!

No phones, no pressure
No deadlines I have to meet
I do my best thinking
When I am off of my feet

I'm just a simple dog
Who always does a flip
Whenever my ears pick up the call
Of a choc-o-late chip
Give me some cookies and tea...and a little T.V.
A simple dog...that's me

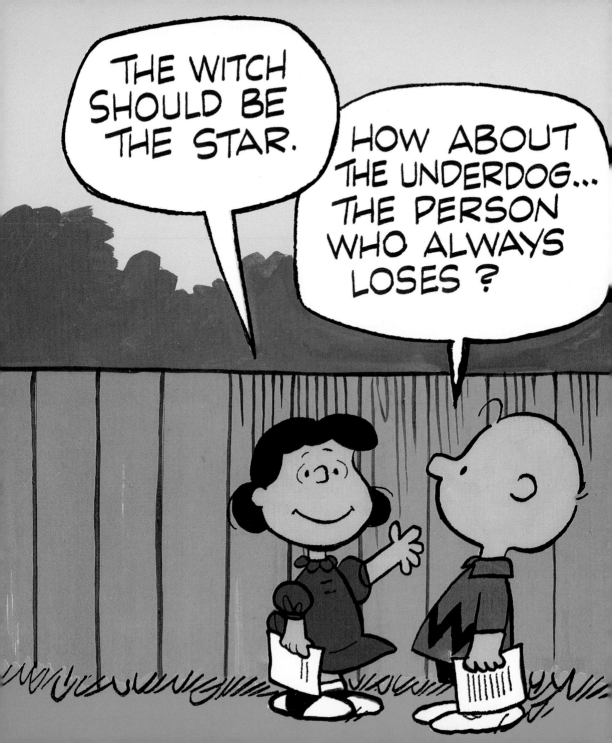

## "We Gotta Get Our Act Together"

We gotta get our act together
We gotta make the pieces fit
Individually we may disagree
But together we'll be a hit…

We gotta form a first-rate unit
We gotta get our team in shape
We gotta get our act together
Then, as one, we will be great!

Somebody said two heads
Are always better than one
So imagine what one, two, three
Four, five could do
We'd be second to none.

The stars and the moon make the heavens
The sunshine and rain make the trees.
So just like the teamwork of nature
Life is a breeze…

# THE
# END